Max & Ruby

THIS BOOK BELONGS TO:

_____

The Max and Ruby Reader Collection

Volume 1

Library and Archives Canada
Cataloguing in Publication

Wells, Rosemary
     The Max and Ruby Reader Collection/
Rosemary Wells, originating author and
illustrator; Harry Endrulat, text adaptation;
illustrations taken from the animated series
Max & Ruby and adapted by Muse
Publishing and Communications Inc.

ISBN 978-1-55470-128-5 (v. 1)

     1. Rabbits – Juvenile fiction.
I. Endrulat, Harry II. Title.

PZ7.W46483Mar 2008   j813'.54
C2008-902245-9

The publisher gratefully acknowledges
the support of the Canada Council for
the Arts and the Ontario Arts Council for
its publishing program. We acknowledge
the support of the Government of Ontario
through the Ontario Media Development
Corporation's Ontario Book Initiative.

We acknowledge the financial support of the
Government of Canada through the Book
Publishing Industry Development Program
(BPIDP) for our publishing activities.

KPk is an imprint of
Key Porter Books Limited
Six Adelaide Street East, Tenth Floor
Toronto, Ontario
Canada M5C 1H6

www.keyporter.com

Book adaptation by
Muse Publishing and Communications Inc.
www.musecommunications.ca

Text adaptation by Harry Endrulat

Printed and bound in China
08 09 10 11 12 6 5 4 3 2 1

Table of Contents

key to reading ™

At Key Porter Kids, we understand how important reading is to a young child's development. That's why we created the Key to Reading program, a structured approach to reading for the beginner. While the books in this series are educational, they are also engaging and fun – key elements in gaining and retaining a child's interest. Plus, with each level in the program designed for different reading abilities, children can advance at their own pace and become successful, confident readers in the process.

Level 1: The Beginner

For children familiar with the alphabet and ready to begin reading.

- Very large type
- Simple words
- Short sentences
- Repetition of key words
- Picture cues
- Colour associations
- Directional reading
- Picture match-up cards

Level 2: The Emerging Reader

For children able to recognize familiar words on sight and sound out new words with help.

- Large type
- Easy words
- Longer sentences
- Repetition of key words and phrases
- Picture cues
- Context cues
- Directional reading
- Picture and word match-up cards

Level 3: The Independent Reader

For increasingly confident readers who can sound out new words on their own.

- Large type
- Expanded vocabulary
- Longer sentences and paragraphs
- Repetition of longer words and phrases
- Picture cues
- Context cues
- More complex storylines
- Flash cards

key to reading
LEVEL 1

Max Meets Morris

Ruby and Louise
were making a sign.

Max and Morris
were playing.

Max loved his yellow truck.
So did Morris.

"Mine," said Morris.
Morris would not share.

Max loved his white ambulance.
So did Morris.

"Mine," said Morris.
Morris would not share.

Max loved his red train.
So did Morris.

"Mine," said Morris.
Morris would not share.

Louise loved the new sign.

So did Ruby.

Max loved his
Jelly Ball Spitting Spider.
So did Morris.

"Mine," said Morris.
A blue jelly ball flew out.

It hit the sign with a...

splash!

**Morris gave Max the
Jelly Ball Spitting Spider.**

A yellow jelly ball flew out.
It hit the sign with a splash!

**Bunny Scout Leader
loved the new sign.**

"Whose idea was it to add
the splashes of colour?"

"Mine," said Max
and Morris together.

Fireman Max

Max was playing fireman.
He wore a red fireman's hat.
He played with a red fire truck.

"Fireman!" said Max.
The fire truck drove away.

Ruby was skipping with Louise.
Ruby jumped and counted.
"One..."

The fire truck drove under Ruby.
"Max," said Ruby.
"Please play somewhere else."

Max played with the white hose.
It was short.

Max found a green hose.
It was long.
"Fireman!" said Max.

Ruby started to skip again.
"One..."

Max bumped into Ruby.
"Max," said Ruby.
"Please play somewhere else."

Max played with the yellow ladder.
It was small.

34

Max found another ladder.
It was tall.
"Fireman!" said Max.

Ruby started to skip again.
"One..."

Max bumped into Louise.
"Max," said Ruby.
"Please play somewhere else."

Max played with the toys
in the sandbox.
They all drove away!

**Bunny Scout Leader came
to watch Ruby.
Ruby got ready to skip.**

The red fire truck
drove toward Ruby.
Ruby skipped: "One!"

The white ambulance
drove toward Ruby.
Ruby skipped again: "Two!"

The black and white police car
drove toward Ruby.
Ruby skipped again: "Three!"

"What a special skipping game,"
said Bunny Scout Leader.
"What do you call it?"

"Fireman!" said Max.

key to reading
LEVEL 1

Max's Work of Art

Ruby and Louise were
painting pictures of fruit.

Max wanted to help.
"Paint," said Max.

Max took Ruby's brush.
He painted the fruit yellow.

"Now we can't paint," said Louise.

"That's okay," said Ruby.
"I know Max can help us."

Ruby helped Max hop onto a table.
He was going to be a model!
Max was happy to help.

53

But he soon got bored.
"Paint," said Max.
He dipped his ship in black paint.

"Why don't we take a break?"
said Ruby. "I'll teach you
about colours, Max."

Ruby mixed red and yellow paint.
They made orange.

She mixed blue and yellow paint.
They made green.

"Okay, Max," said Ruby.
"Let's finish your picture."
Max hopped back onto the table.

Ruby and Louise finished
Max's painting. They went
inside to clean up.

Max still wanted to play with colours.
"Paint," he said.

But he didn't know what to paint.
Then Max got an idea.

Ruby and Louise went outside.
Grandma was there.

"I love all three paintings," she said.
"But we only painted two," said Ruby.

"And Max's painting," said Grandma.

"What did Max paint?" asked Ruby.

"Me," said Max.

key to reading
LEVEL 2

Max Is It

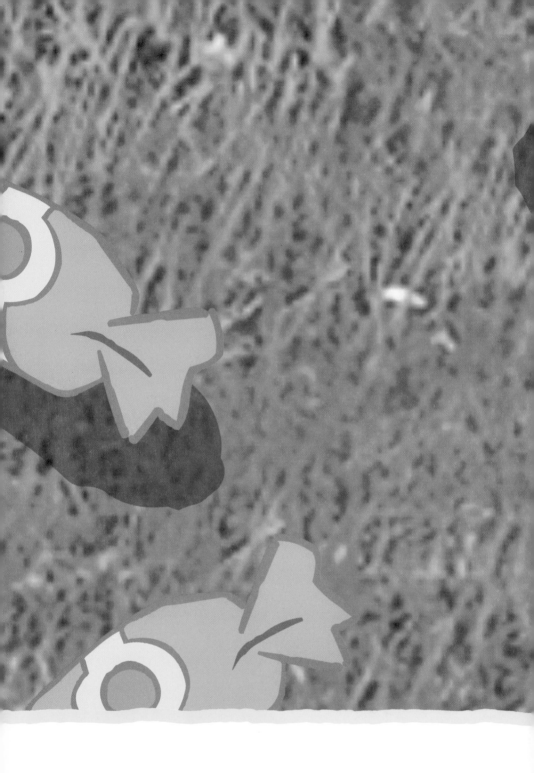

Max was hungry.

He wanted a Slime Dribbler candy.

To get it, Max had to play freeze tag
with Valerie, Louise and Ruby.

"Catch us if you can, Max," said Ruby.

Max chased Valerie, Louise and Ruby.
They were too fast.

Max got an idea.

Max hid at the top of the slide.
He waited for Valerie to walk by.

Then he slid down and tagged her.
"Freeze!" said Max.

Max chased Louise and Ruby
around the teeter-totter.
They were too fast.

Max got an idea.

Max didn't run around the teeter-totter.

He ran across it and tagged Louise.
"Freeze!" said Max.

Max chased Ruby.
She was too fast.

Max got an idea.

Max hid at the top of the slide again.
He waited for Ruby to walk by.

Then he slid down and tagged her.
"Freeze!" said Max.

Valerie, Louise and Ruby were frozen.
They could not move.

Max reached into Ruby's backpack.

"Dribbler!" said Max.

Ruby Writes a Story

Max was playing cowboy.

Ruby was trying to write a story.
"Once upon a time, there was a..."

"Cowboy!" yelled Max.
Max played a song on his
silver harmonica.

"I'm sorry, Max," said Ruby.
"I can't play cowboy now.
I'm trying to write a story."

Max played cowboy
with his yellow chicks.

Ruby started her story again.
"Once upon a time, there was a..."

"Cowboy!" yelled Max.
Max herded the yellow chicks
through the kitchen.

"I'm sorry, Max," said Ruby.
"I can't play cowboy now.
I'm trying to write a story."

Max played cowboy
with his red lobster.

Ruby started her story again.
"Once upon a time, there was a..."

"Cowboy!" yelled Max.
Max lassoed his red lobster.

"I'm sorry, Max," said Ruby.
"I'm trying to write a story,
but you keep interrupting."

"First, you played your harmonica.
Next, you herded your yellow chicks
through the kitchen."

"Then, you lassoed your red lobster.
No wonder I can't think of what
comes next in my story."

"I only get to start my story:
Once upon a time, there was a..."

"Cowboy!" yelled Max.

"That's it, Max!" said Ruby.
"I know what to write.
And you can help me."

Ruby started her story again:
"Once upon a time, there was a..."

"Cowboy!" yelled Max,
finishing the first line of Ruby's story.

Max &
Ruby

Super Max
Saves the World

Max and Morris were
playing superheroes.

Max was Super Bunny.
Morris was Zoom Zoom.

Ruby and Louise were blowing up balloons. There was a small yellow one, a big blue one and an even bigger red one.

Ruby hit the red balloon.
It floated away!
"Uh-oh," said Ruby.

Max zoomed into the kitchen.
He caught the red balloon.
"Super Bunny!" said Max.

Morris zoomed into the kitchen.
"Zoom Zoom!" said Morris.

Ruby took the red balloon back.
"We need these balloons," she said.
"We're making a solar system."

"The smallest balloon is going
to be the moon," said Louise.
Ruby pointed to a picture of the moon.

"The bigger balloon is going
to be the earth," said Louise.
Ruby pointed to a picture of the earth.

"The biggest balloon is going
to be the sun," said Louise.
Ruby pointed to a picture of the sun.

123

"Now please zoom away," said Ruby.
"We don't want you to break the balloons."

"Super Bunny!" said Max.
"Zoom Zoom!" said Morris.
Together they zoomed away.

Ruby and Louise glued paper to the balloons.
Some paper got glued to their faces!

Ruby and Louise painted the moon grey.
They painted the sun yellow.
They painted the earth blue and green.

Ruby tried to put the earth on a hanger.
But she tripped over Max's red lobster.
The earth went flying in the air!

Max and Morris zoomed into the kitchen.
Max caught the earth!
"Super Bunny!" said Max.

"Thank you, Super Bunny," said Ruby.
"Thank you, Zoom Zoom," said Louise.

"You saved…"

"The world!" said Max.

CUT ALONG DOTTED LINES

CUT ALONG DOTTED LINES

CUT ALONG DOTTED LINES

✂

CUT ALONG DOTTED LINES

Max

Max

Bug

Bug

Ruby

Ruby

Louise

Louise

Valerie

Valerie

Dribbler

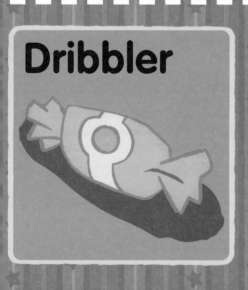

Dribbler

Max

Max

Lobster

Lobster

Chicks

Chicks

Ruby

Ruby

Hat

Hat

Horse

Horse

Max

Max

Ruby

Ruby

Balloon

Balloon

Louise

Louise

Morris

Morris

Earth

Earth